50006630

D1280311

A Note to Parents and Caregivers:

Read-it! Readers are for children who are just starting on the amazing road to reading. These beautiful books support both the acquisition of reading skills and the love of books.

The RED LEVEL presents familiar topics using common words and repeating sentence patterns.
The BLUE LEVEL presents new ideas using a larger vocabulary and varied sentence structure.
The YELLOW LEVEL presents more challenging ideas, a broad vocabulary, and wide variety in sentence structure.

When sharing a book with your child, read in short stretches, pausing often to talk about the pictures. Have your child turn the pages and point to the pictures and familiar words. And be sure to reread favorite stories or parts of stories.

There is no right or wrong way to share books with children. Find time to read with your child and pass on the legacy of literacy.

Adria F. Klein, Ph.D.
Professor Emeritus
California State University
San Bernardino, California

First American edition published in 2003 by
Picture Window Books
5115 Excelsior Boulevard
Suite 232
Minneapolis, MN 55416
1-877-845-8392
www.picturewindowbooks.com

First published in Great Britain by Franklin Watts, 96 Leonard Street, London, EC2A 4XD
Text © Anne Cassidy 2000
Illustration © Lisa Smith 2000

Printed in the United States of America.
1 2 3 4 5 6 08 07 06 05 04 03

Library of Congress Cataloging-in-Publication Data
Cassidy, Anne, 1952-
[Cheeky Monkey]
  The sassy monkey / written by Anne Cassidy ; illustrated by Lisa Smith.—1st American ed.
    p. cm. — (Read-it! readers)
Originally published: London :F.Watts, c2000, under title: Cheeky monkey.
  Summary: When Wendy finds a monkey in her treehouse, she tries a number of ways to rid
of him.
  ISBN 1-4048-0058-1
  [1. Monkeys—Fiction. 2. Tree houses—Fiction.] I. Smith, Lisa, ill. II. Title. III. Series.
  PZ7.C26857 Sas 2003
  [E]—dc21   2002074945

PICTURE WINDOW BOOKS

Read-it! Readers
Blue Level

The Sassy Monkey

Written by Anne Cassidy

Illustrated by Lisa Smith

Reading Advisors:
Adria F. Klein, Ph.D.
Professor Emeritus, California State University
San Bernardino, California

Ruth Thomas
Durham Public Schools
Durham, North Carolina

R. Ernice Bookout
Durham Public Schools
Durham, North Carolina

Picture Window Books
Minneapolis, Minnesota

Wendy woke up late one day.

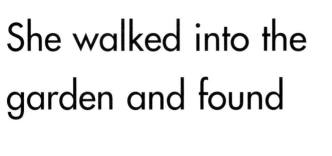

She walked into the
garden and found

a monkey sitting in
her tree house.

"Monkey, get out of my tree house!" Wendy shouted.

"No, I'm staying here!"
the monkey shouted back.

Wendy turned purple
with anger.

"Oh no you're not!"
she shouted.

Wendy made a plan.

She went into battle with the monkey.

But the monkey had
custard pies.

"Take that!" he shouted
as he threw them at Wendy.

Wendy needed a new plan.

She took a look in her
toy box.

Wendy became a pirate.

She made a plan to take over the tree house.

The monkey became a
pirate, too.

He shot hundreds of peanuts
to keep Wendy away.

So Wendy became
a cowgirl.

She made a plan to
catch the monkey.

But the monkey had a
better plan, and Wendy
got very wet.

The monkey laughed and laughed.

Wendy made another plan.

She went into the kitchen.

Wendy made a trap for
the monkey.

He came straight down
from the tree house—

and got straight into
Wendy's bed!

Red Level

The Best Snowman, by Margaret Nash 1-4048-0048-4
Bill's Baggy Pants, by Susan Gates 1-4048-0050-6
Cleo and Leo, by Anne Cassidy 1-4048-0049-2
Felix on the Move, by Maeve Friel 1-4048-0055-7
Jasper and Jess, by Anne Cassidy 1-4048-0061-1
The Lazy Scarecrow, by Jillian Powell 1-4048-0062-X
Little Joe's Big Race, by Andy Blackford 1-4048-0063-8
The Little Star, by Deborah Nash 1-4048-0065-4
The Naughty Puppy, by Jillian Powell 1-4048-0067-0
Selfish Sophie, by Damian Kelleher 1-4048-0069-7

Blue Level

The Bossy Rooster, by Margaret Nash 1-4048-0051-4
Jack's Party, by Ann Bryant 1-4048-0060-3
Little Red Riding Hood, by Maggie Moore 1-4048-0064-6
Recycled!, by Jillian Powell 1-4048-0068-9
The Sassy Monkey, by Anne Cassidy 1-4048-0058-1
The Three Little Pigs, by Maggie Moore 1-4048-0071-9

Yellow Level

Cinderella, by Barrie Wade 1-4048-0052-2
The Crying Princess, by Anne Cassidy 1-4048-0053-0
Eight Enormous Elephants, by Penny Dolan 1-4048-0054-9
Freddie's Fears, by Hilary Robinson 1-4048-0056-5
Goldilocks and the Three Bears, by Barrie Wade 1-4048-0057-3
Mary and the Fairy, by Penny Dolan 1-4048-0066-2
Jack and the Beanstalk, by Maggie Moore 1-4048-0059-X
The Three Billy Goats Gruff, by Barrie Wade 1-4048-0070-0